SWEET DREAMS PRESS
SHREWSBURY, NJ 07702

VISIT US AT WWW.NIGHTSPRYTES.COM

ISBN 0-9677238-8-4

BEDTIME
WITH
ROLLO

BY

DAVID BIER

SETH BIER

SWEET DREAMS PRESS

AN IMPRINT OF BIER BROS., INC.
SHREWSBURY, NJ

To Mom and Dad,
For always keeping
the monsters
away

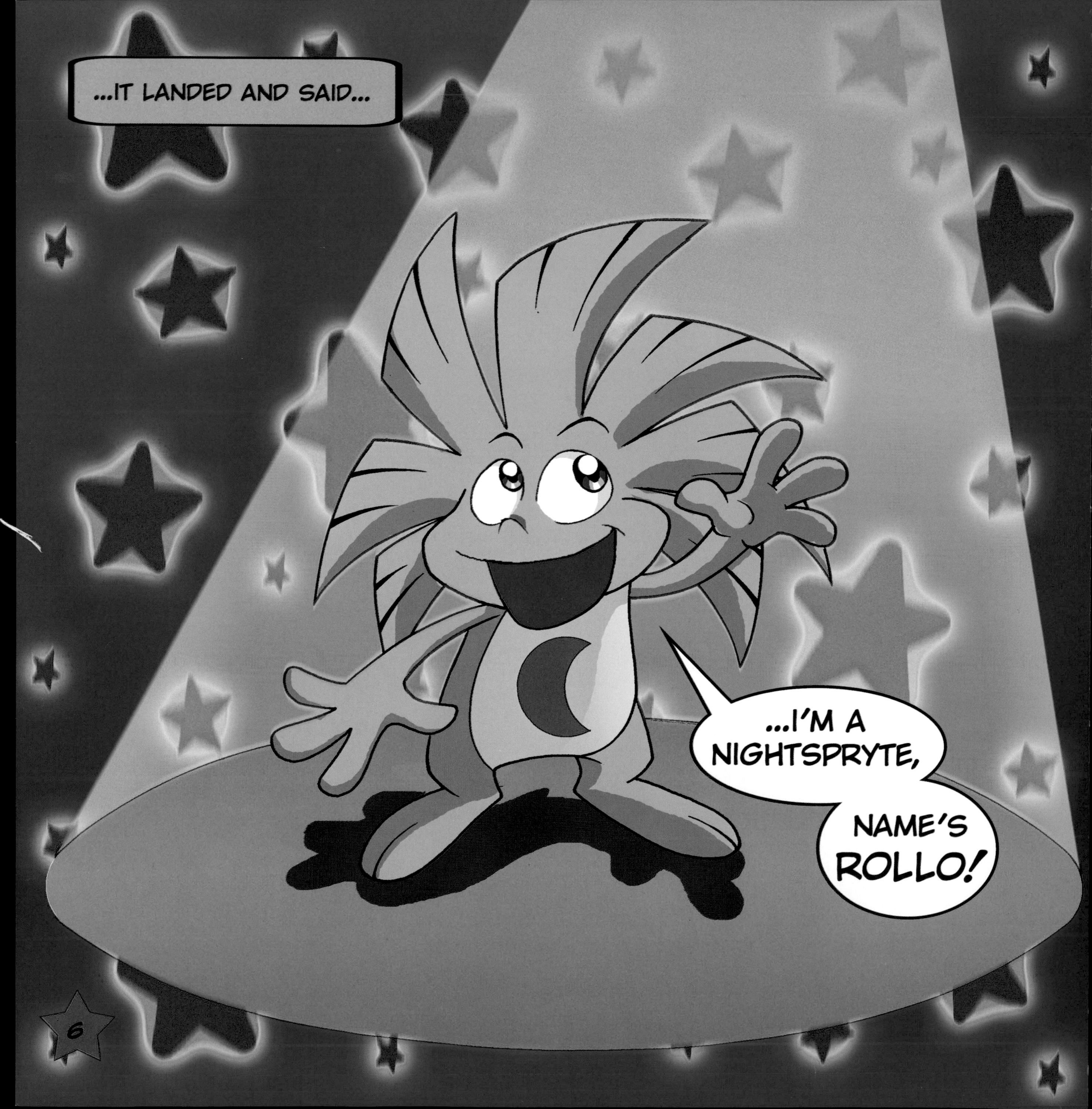
...IT LANDED AND SAID...
...I'M A NIGHTSPRYTE,
NAME'S ROLLO!

THEY LOOKED IN THE CLOSET AND IN THERE THEY FOUND

A WHOLE BUNCH OF MONSTERS JUST HANGING AROUND.

THIS WOULD EXPLAIN YOUR BEDTIME ANXIETY.

THERE'S MONSTERS IN ALMOST EVERY VARIETY.